THE BEASTLY VISITS

by Mitra Modarressi

ORCHARD BOOKS

New York

Orchard Books, 95 Madison Avenue, New York, NY 10016

Manufactured in the United States of America. Printed by Barton Press, Inc. Bound by Horowitz/Rae.
Book design by Jean Krulis. The text of this book is set in 16 point Usherwood Book.
The illustrations are watercolor reproduced in full color.

1   3   5   7   9   10   8   6   4   2

Library of Congress Cataloging-in-Publication Data
Modarressi, Mitra. The beastly visits / by Mitra Modarressi. p.   cm. Summary: Newton is a small,
curious monster who befriends Miles, a boy accustomed to being alone, and shows him that
friends not only play together but also stick up for one another.
ISBN 0-531-09530-4. — ISBN 0-531-08880-4 (lib. bdg.)
[1. Friendship—Fiction.   2. Monsters—Fiction.   3. Bullies—Fiction.]   I. Title.
PZ7.M7137Be   1996   [E]—dc20   96-1953

For GREG

There was once a small monster named Newton who lived with his parents in a burrow beneath an old house.

A secret passageway led up through the house to the room
of a boy named Miles. Miles didn't know about Newton,
but Newton knew all about Miles because he loved to peek
out at him. He liked watching Miles play with his crayons
and his train set and his baseball cards and his jigsaw
puzzles. Miles spent a lot of time in his room.

Newton wished he and Miles could be friends. "Why don't you go play with him?" his mother asked.

"Oh, I couldn't," Newton said. But that night he tiptoed up
the stairs and opened the door.
The hinges went *screeeek*. Miles gave a yell, and Newton
was so startled that he slammed the door shut and ran
back down the stairs.

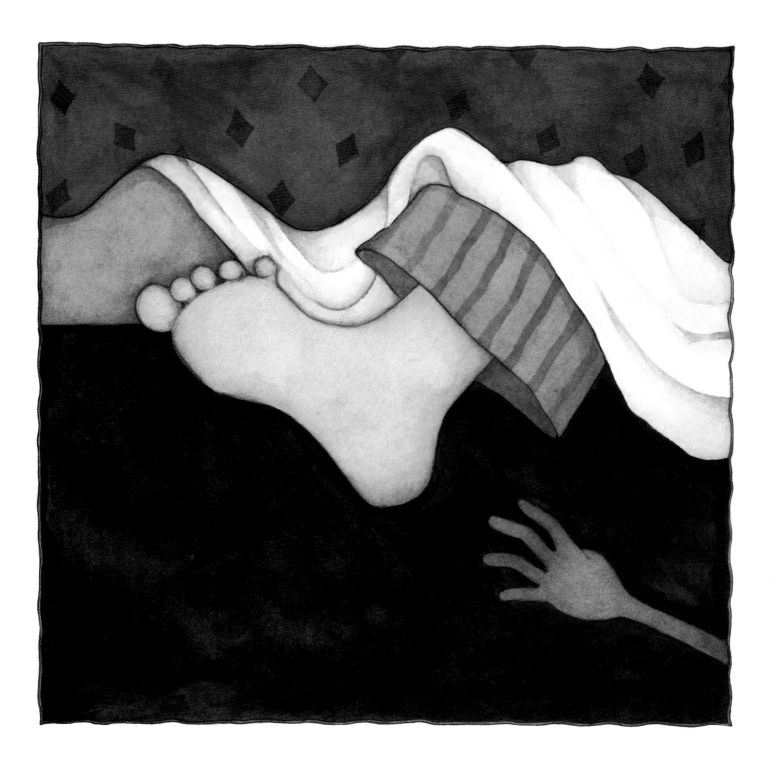

But the next night, Newton tried again. Slowly, he opened the door so it wouldn't creak. Gently, he poked Miles's foot as it dangled over the side of the bed. "Yikes!" Miles said, and jumped up and ran out of the room.

Newton felt very discouraged. His father said, "Don't be so shy. Just speak up and introduce yourself!"

Newton decided to be braver. The following afternoon, he marched to the top of the stairs and flung the door open. Out he came from under the bed. "Hi!" he said. "I'm Newton." Miles's eyes grew as big as saucers. "I'm—I'm—Miles," he said in a very small voice.

"Excuse me," Newton apologized, "but my mother said
maybe we could play together."

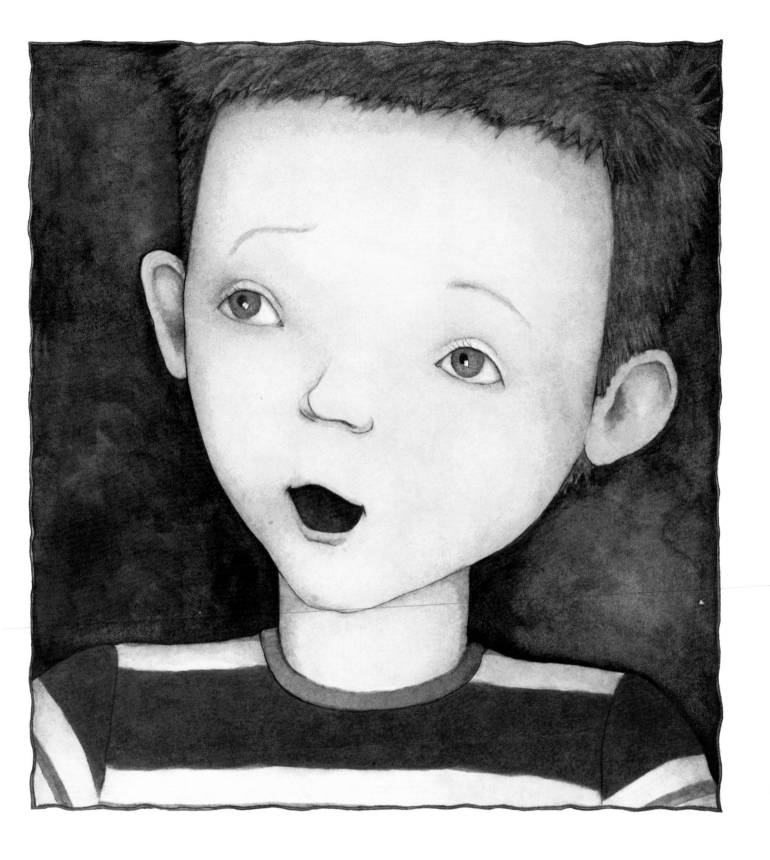

Miles looked shocked. "You have a mother?"

"Of course I do," Newton said, "and a father, too. Would you like to meet them?"
Miles thought for a moment. "Are they nice?"
"They're *very* nice," Newton said.
So they went back through the door and down the stairs.

Newton's parents were pleased to see Miles. They tried to make him feel at home.

Miles and Newton played Newton's favorite game, Climbing
Father's Scales.

Later, Newton's mother served cobweb candy, which Miles politely declined.

When Miles left, Newton's parents invited him to come back anytime.

Miles and Newton began to play together almost every day.

One day, while they were building a fort in Miles's room,
Newton said, "Why don't we show this to some of your
friends?"
Miles looked worried. He said, "I don't think that's such a
good idea."

The next afternoon, while they were trading comic books,
Newton said, "Let's ask a couple of your friends to bring
their comic books over."
Miles said, "Oh, maybe someday."

But Newton didn't want to wait. He decided to follow Miles to see what his other friends were like.

The place Miles went looked like fun. But Miles was standing all by himself.
Then a big, mean-looking kid walked over to Miles, grabbed his hat, and said, "This is *my* hat now!"

Newton's eyes reddened, and his hair stood on end. He came out of hiding to stand beside Miles. "Newton!" Miles exclaimed. "What are you doing here?" The bully sneered, "Hey, Miles, who's your stupid-looking friend?"

Miles stepped right up to the bully and looked him in the eye.
"Don't make fun of my friend," he said, and snatched his hat back.

The bully gulped and slunk away.

From then on, Miles had many friends. And so did Newton.
He was especially popular at Halloween.

Miles's parents were a little surprised when they first met Newton.
When they got to know him, though, they thought that he was
wonderful.

They asked him over for dinner and served Miles's favorite
dish, pizza, which Newton politely declined.